A Nightmare

"I think it looks pretty good for a house that's been around for over a hundred years," Dr. Beekman said cheerfully.

"The inside's worse than the outside!" Kate groaned, letting her blankets fall to the floor in despair.

Mrs. Beekman shone the flashlight around the living room. It lit up curtains of spider webs hanging from the ceiling and a pile of dead leaves spilling out of the fireplace. There was a puddle of dirty water on the floor underneath one of the broken windows.

"Is this a nightmare or what?" demanded Kate.

"Can you believe anyone ever actually *lived* here?" Stephanie murmured to me

Trying to be encouraging, Patti said, "It's a little like camping out."

Look for these and other books
in the Sleepover Friends Series:

Kate's Camp-Out

Susan Saunders

AN
APPLE
PAPERBACK

SCHOLASTIC INC.
New York Toronto London Auckland Sydney

ISBN 0-590-41337-6

12 11 10 9 8 7 6 5 4 3   8 9/8 0 1 2 3/9

Printed in the U.S.A.   28

First Scholastic printing, June 1988

Chapter
1

"This reminds me of a late movie I once saw: *Journey to the Center of the Earth* . . . only I think we passed the center about an hour ago, and now we're headed for China!" Kate Beekman peered through the windshield from the front seat of the car. Stephanie Green, Patti Jenkins, and I — I'm Lauren Hunter — were squashed together behind her in the backseat.

It was Friday night. Normally, the four of us would have been comfortably settled in at one of our houses, scarfing down junk food and maybe listening to requests on WBRM Riverhurst: the beginning of a typical Friday-night sleepover. Instead, Mrs. Beekman was driving us upstate, to a cabin on Spirit Lake, where we were going to spend the whole weekend!

"Just how much farther is this place?" Kate asked her mother for the fifth time.

"Kate, do you realize you're beginning to sound an awful lot like your little sister?" Mrs. Beekman spun the steering wheel sharply to the left, but she couldn't dodge the huge pothole in the narrow road. The car's right front tire dropped into it with a clunk that rattled the box of pots and pans in the trunk, and bounced us around like marbles.

"Ouch!" Stephanie squawked. "Wow! Do you have a hard head, Patti!" She rubbed her dark curls with her hand.

Patti's the tallest and thinnest girl in our class — I guess her head is as bony as the rest of her. "Sorry," she apologized, scrunching her lanky frame closer to the door to give Stephanie more room.

The backseat of the Beekmans' family car usually holds three of us with room to spare, but that night we were sharing it with two sleeping bags and all the groceries that wouldn't fit in the trunk or in Kate's dad's little car.

"It's already been three hours," Kate murmured, checking her watch by the glow of the dashboard. "To get to the middle of nowhere, only to have the Norwood boys breathing down our necks! Why didn't you tell me they have a place on the lake?"

"Daddy's been so busy, he didn't think to mention it. Besides, you haven't seen Sam and Dave since the hospital picnic, Kate," Mrs. Beekman said. "Boys change quickly at eight or nine — I'm sure they're much more mature. And Dr. Norwood said they'd be glad to take you fishing or hiking, or lend you their boat."

"I'm not letting those brats get anywhere near Lauren and Patti and Stephanie — they'd never forgive me," Kate declared. "Sam and Dave are fiends!"

"Maybe they *have* changed," I told her. "Remember how awful Henry Larkin was in second grade, always playing tricks on the girls?" Henry Larkin is a boy in our class. "By the end of third grade, he actually got cute."

"It'll never happen to the Norwoods," Kate said gloomily. "Minds capable of dreaming up water pistols filled with disappearing ink are capable of anything!"

Sam and Dave Norwood don't live in our town, but Dr. Norwood works at the same hospital as Kate's dad, which is why Kate met them at the hospital picnic.

"I almost died when they squirted me," she went on. "Big blue blobs of ink all over my new yellow jumpsuit! I yelled my head off! And then the stuff disappeared, so everybody thought I was crazy! I've never been so embarrassed in my life!"

"Don't worry, we'll protect you from the Norwoods," Stephanie said.

"I don't need protection from the Norwoods. I need protection from myself!" Kate exclaimed. "If they start up with me again, I'll — I'll try to strangle them, and *I'll* end up in jail!"

A weekend at Spirit Lake had sounded great when Kate told us about it at Patti's sleepover the week before: an old cabin next to the water, walks in the woods, cookouts. . . .

"I love the country," Patti had said. "I'll ask my parents right away!"

"I'm sure Mom and Dad'll say okay," I told Kate. "And they'll take care of Fredericka, too." Fredericka is Kate's kitten, sister to my Rocky, and Stephanie's Cinders, and Patti's Adelaide.

"Terrific!" Kate said. "What about you, Stephanie?"

"Well, I'm not wild about bugs . . . or outdoor animals . . . and stuff," said Stephanie. "But I'm not going to sit at home while you guys have fun. Count me in, too."

So there we were, wherever *that* was. We did seem to be in the middle of nowhere. We hadn't

4

seen a house since the last little town. Dark pine trees loomed over the road on both sides of the car, blocking out the sky. It was like driving down a tunnel with no exit.

My stomach rumbled loudly. "I guess I'm hungry," I admitted. I'd had a sandwich before I went to Kate's house late that afternoon, but that was ages earlier.

"You're always hungry," Kate said. I *do* have a healthy appetite.

"Look through the groceries, Lauren," Mrs. Beekman suggested. "Is there anything you can snack on?"

I felt around in the dark, hoping for a bag of cookies, or at least some chips, but all I came up with was two cans of Comet, a king-size bottle of Mr. Clean, and a package of rubber gloves. "That's okay, Mrs. Beekman. I can wait."

"*Eeeeuuu!* What was that?" Stephanie squealed as something with scraggly gray fur and a long pink tail scuttled across the road in front of us, its eyes gleaming in the car's headlights. "It looked like a monster rat!"

"City girls!" Kate sniffed. "It was only a possum."

"Gross me out!" Stephanie muttered.

"Maybe we missed the turn, Mom," Kate said then. "We could be miles out of our way." She looked at the three of us in the backseat and added glumly, "You're probably all thinking I'm a jerk for dragging you along. What if this turns out to be the worst sleepover ever?"

Actually, I *had* been thinking about how good the take-out egg rolls are at Szechuan Empire in Riverhurst. But how bad could a sleepover with Kate be? She and I have a history: We've been having sleepovers at each other's houses since we were five!

Kate and I aren't anything alike: she's blonde, and I have dark brown hair. She's pretty serious, I'm sometimes almost too easygoing. She's incredibly neat, I was *born* messy. But we've been best friends for years.

We live practically next door to each other on Pine Street, so we played together constantly when we were little kids. By the time we were in kindergarten at Riverhurst Elementary, we'd started taking turns sleeping over on Friday nights — that's when Kate's dad named us the Sleepover Twins.

We'd dress up in our mothers' clothes and shoes and pretend to be grown-ups, or make ice pops in ice-cube trays, with cherry Kool-Aid and Dr. Beekman's tongue depressors — we called that "cooking."

We moved on to better things as we got older, like my special invention: onion-soup-olives-bacon-bits-and-sour-cream dip with barbecue potato chips, and Kate's super marshmallow fudge. We watched every movie on Friday-night TV because Kate wants to be a director some day, played about a million games of Truth or Dare, and wrote our own Mad Libs. There was my older brother, Roger, to spy on when he got interesting, and Melissa, Kate's little sister, to avoid at her house when she got tiresome, which was most of the time. But it was basically just the two of us, Kate and me.

Just before fourth grade, Stephanie moved from the city to a house not far down on Pine Street. She and I were both in Mr. Civello's fourth-grade class — that's where we got to be friends.

When I get up in the morning, I put on a sweatshirt and jeans without thinking about it that much, right? Not Stephanie. She already has a definite style. For instance, most of her clothes — and even her room — are in her favorite color combination: red, black, and white. She's always thinking of fun stuff to do, like copying new hairstyles from teen maga-

7

zines or trying out dance routines to music videos. And I love hearing about her life back in the city. I invited Stephanie to a Friday sleepover at my house because I wanted her and Kate to be friends, too.

But Kate and Stephanie didn't hit it off right away. In fact, sometimes they still have problems getting along.

"They're too much alike," my brother Roger says. "Both bossy!" Until this year, I found myself caught in the middle lots of times. But things changed when Patti Jenkins turned up in Mrs. Mead's fifth-grade class last September.

Patti's one of those people who never forgets anything she's read or heard, so she gets terrific grades. Tall and quiet and shy, she couldn't be more different from Stephanie, who's short and outgoing and talkative. You'd never know it, but Patti's from the city, too. She and Stephanie even went to the same school in kindergarten and first grade!

Stephanie wanted Patti to be part of our group, which was fine with Kate and me because we liked Patti right away. With her around to balance things out, Kate and Stephanie finally settled down, and now there are four Sleepover Friends — all for one, and one for all. We could definitely handle the Norwoods!

Stephanie, Patti, and I hung on as Mrs. Beekman veered around a patch of loose gravel. "It's going to be a great sleepover, Kate," Patti said soothingly.

"It'll be different, that's for sure," Stephanie whispered in my ear. "The first sleepover we've ever spent in a moving car."

"What's so funny?" Kate demanded from the front seat when Stephanie and I giggled.

Before we had to come up with an answer, Mrs. Beekman's headlights shone on the back of a red car. "There they are!" she said with a sigh of relief.

Dr. Beekman's VW Rabbit was parked on the side of the road, next to an open gate with a wooden sign hanging from it: Spirit Lake Cottages. Kate's dad and Melissa were sitting on the fence — they waved excitedly as we pulled up next to them and piled out.

"We saw a deer, and a raccoon, and an owl!" Melissa screeched, practically jumping up and down. "Bet *you* didn't!"

"We saw a giant rat," said Stephanie, peering down at the ground as if she expected one to run across her feet at any second.

"Isn't this fantastic?" Dr. Beekman's widespread arms took in the trees, the moon and stars, and probably the deer and the rats as well. "Just like it was when I was a kid and used to camp around here with my granddad!"

"It's quite a long drive, Morris," Mrs. Beekman replied cautiously, shivering in the cool night air.

"It may be a little far for an average weekend," Dr. Beekman admitted. "But maybe I can talk Charlie Porter into renting it to us for two or three weeks this summer. Since he bought that condo in the mountains, he doesn't really use his place on the lake very much." Dr. Beekman clapped his hands together. "Well, gang — what are we waiting for?" He and Melissa jumped back into the little red car. "Follow us!"

The two cars rolled through the gate, crept up a winding dirt road, and finally came out of the forest at the edge of Spirit Lake. It was a huge circle of water, sparkling in the moonlight. There must have been fifty cottages strung out along the shore. Lights shone in just a few of them.

"Nice houses!" said Patti. "I like the one with the slanted roof and all the skylights."

"Look — that one has a round deck on top for sunbathing," Stephanie pointed out. "And a hot tub! I wonder what Dr. Porter's house is like."

"I wonder if he has cable TV," Kate added.

"There's a great movie on *Thriller Theater* at midnight — *The Beast with Six Fingers*."

We didn't have to wonder long. Dr. Beekman stopped at a brown mailbox in the shape of a duck and climbed out of his car. "Here we are!" he announced, checking the number on the gate. "Forty-nine Lake Drive."

Stephanie gave a low whistle.

Kate slowly opened her car door. "You have *got* to be kidding," she said.

Chapter 2

It was dark of course, but we could see more than enough, even though the yard was overgrown with bushes and weeds. The Porter house was a two-story shingled box covered with flaking paint. The second story seemed to be leaning a little, the roof definitely looked saggy on the chimney end, and two of the four small windows in front had broken panes.

"Oh, Morris," Mrs. Beekman whispered. "When was the last time Charlie Porter was here?"

"I've seen this place before," Kate said grimly.

"You have?" Dr. Beekman sounded puzzled.

"Yeah, it's where the Gruesomes spend their summer vacation!" *The Gruesomes* is that TV show about the weird family: The father's a vampire, the mother's a monster, the aunt's a witch, the older boy's a werewolf, and they live in a haunted castle.

Melissa shrieked, which made Patti and me jump. We giggled nervously.

"I think it looks pretty good for a house that's been around for over a hundred years," Dr. Beekman said cheerfully. "You'll like it when we get the lights on."

He reached under the front seat of his car for a big flashlight. Then he headed up the sidewalk to the front door. He pulled some keys out of his pocket, and we could hear him fiddling with the locks. There was a click, and the door swung open.

"Here's the light switch," he reported to us over his shoulder. "I'm turning it on. . . ."

Nothing happened!

"Morris?" Mrs. Beekman called.

"The bulb's probably burned out," Dr. Beekman reassured us. "I'll just step inside. . . ." He disappeared into the creepy old house.

A minute passed, then two. "Where is he?" Mrs. Beekman asked. "I'd better go see if he needs help."

But Dr. Beekman reappeared at the front door just then, his flashlight still on. "There's a little problem," he said, sounding a lot less cheerful. "None of the lights are working — no electricity." He shook his head. "I can't understand it. I called a Mr. Morrell in Ansonville" — that was the little town we'd driven through last — "and asked him to turn the electricity on, along with the water. . . ."

"Oh, dear — no water, either?" said Mrs. Beekman.

"The pump is electric," said Dr. Beekman.

Stephanie groaned softly. "How am I supposed to do my beauty regimen?" she whispered to me. She'd been washing her face with three kinds of special oils and then steaming it with hot water. "Ignore your pores, and you're in big trouble," she says.

"I got Morrell's name from Charlie. He told me Morrell would come out Thursday morning and take care of everything," Dr. Beekman went on.

"Then he'll just have to come now," Mrs. Beekman said firmly.

"No phone, remember?" said Dr. Beekman. "And the Norwoods are on the other side of the lake. It's too late to bother them anyway." He threw up his hands. "I give up — let's check into a motel."

"Where? I didn't notice a motel in Ansonville," Mrs. Beekman said. She was starting to sound a little cranky.

"I'm starving!" Melissa whined. "Couldn't we make some hot dogs in the fireplace?"

"For once, I agree with the kid," Kate said.

"Everyone's too hungry and tired to chase all over the country looking for a motel," Mrs. Beekman told her husband. "We'll have to make the best of it for tonight, and call Mr. Morrell early in the morning."

Dr. Beekman nodded. "Okay. I'll find some dry wood, and get a fire going in the fireplace."

The circle of bright light from his flashlight bobbed across the yard as he pushed his way through the bushes and weeds to the back of the house.

"All right, girls," Mrs. Beekman said wearily. "Everybody grab something from the cars and carry it inside. The sooner we unpack, the sooner we eat. And the sooner we go to bed!" she added to herself.

Mrs. Beekman took a small flashlight out of the glove compartment of her car and opened both trunks. I picked up a sleeping bag and a bag of groceries, Kate grabbed a pile of blankets, Stephanie reached for the box of pots and pans, Patti carried our backpacks, and Melissa took some pillows.

"Do you think there are snakes?" Patti whispered.

I shook my head, but I wasn't so sure. Who knew what was lurking in the weeds? They were tall enough to hide a moose, or even a grizzly! I knew what Kate would say if she could read my thoughts: "You're letting your imagination run away with you again, Lauren."

We stumbled in a hurry up the uneven sidewalk behind Mrs. Beekman and through the front door.

"The inside's worse than the outside!" Kate groaned, letting her blankets fall to the floor in despair.

Mrs. Beekman shone the flashlight around the living room. It lit up curtains of spider webs hanging from the ceiling, and a pile of dead leaves spilling out of the fireplace. There was a puddle of dirty water on the floor underneath one of the broken windows, and mice had pulled the stuffing out of a couch. Kate hates it when things aren't neat, and this place was terminal.

Dr. Beekman clumped in with an armload of wood and a kerosene lantern. "I found this by the door," he told us, swinging the lantern. "And there's a woodpile out back." He arranged the smaller pieces of wood on the bottom of the fireplace, placed a larger log on top, and struck a match, which he also used to light the lantern. "And there's an outdoor toilet left over from the old days, too, so we're all set until tomorrow."

"Is this a nightmare or what?" demanded Kate, who likes things to go smoothly.

16

"You have to go *outdoors* to use outdoor toilets," Stephanie murmured to me. "Can you believe anyone ever actually *lived* here?"

"It's a little like camping out," Patti said, trying to be encouraging.

When the fire stopped sputtering and caught, all of us felt better.

"Lauren, the hot dogs are in the brown paper bag," Mrs. Beekman said. "And the buns are in the box of groceries on the floor, Stephanie."

Kate and Patti set a long rickety table with paper plates and cups, while Kate's dad went outside again to cut branches from a tree growing next to the house. We stripped the leaves off and used the sticks to roast our hot dogs on.

Mrs. Beekman had brought mustard and pickle relish and chips and Dr Peppers — no ice, but warm DP is better than no DP at all. The hot dogs were great: smoky-tasting from the fire, crisp on the outside and steaming on the inside. I ate three of them, and half a bag of sour-cream-and-onion potato chips. Then we roasted marshmallows, holding them over the coals until they'd almost melted, and ate them off the sticks. And that wasn't all — Kate had a container filled with super-fudge in her backpack.

"All ri-i-ight!" exclaimed Stephanie, grabbing two big chunks.

"All the comforts of home," said Dr. Beekman, snaring a piece, too. He'd been upstairs, exploring the second floor. "Three bedrooms, with two cots in each. I know how you girls like your privacy, so you can have the whole floor to yourselves — I lit a kerosene lantern for you."

"What about me, Daddy?" Melissa piped up.

"You'll stay in the bedroom down here with us, sweetie," said Dr. Beekman. "Leave the big girls alone, for once."

That would have been great news any other time, but *that* night, in *that* house I was thinking about safety in numbers. Patti and Stephanie and I stared uneasily at the steep stairs leading to the second floor, and then at Kate. Stephanie was probably thinking about rats, but now my mind was running along creepier lines. I wondered who *had* lived there before, as in old house . . . old *ghosts*.

Dr. Beekman took another piece of fudge on his way toward the back door. "I'm going to fill a bucket down at the lake. We'll boil the water for some tooth-brushing and face-washing before we turn in."

"Not yet, Dad, okay? We're not sleepy," Kate said. "Why don't we sit around, finish the fudge, talk

18

for a while? You can tell us about this place."

"Yes, Dr. Beekman, like why it's called Spirit Lake," said Stephanie.

Dr. Beekman sat down on the mouse-eaten couch next to Mrs. Beekman and Melissa. The rest of us were leaning against the luggage; Patti and Stephanie had pulled their sleeping bags up around their shoulders.

"Well, there are several stories about that," Dr. Beekman began. "And one of them is a little spooky."

Spooky? A chill ran down my spine.

"It has to do with two fur trappers named Willis Pyle and Roy Jonas," Dr. Beekman went on. "They had cabins on opposite sides of the lake. This area was great for trapping in those days — beavers, foxes, even bears. Willis was lucky — he'd end up with hundreds of pelts. But Roy's traps would break, or he'd catch a silver fox and a bear would eat it before he could save the fur.

"As the story goes, Willis made a lot of money. He spent it, too, on a fancy rifle with a carved stock and silver inlays in the barrel, and a diamond ring, and a high-stepping gray horse. Roy, on the other hand, barely scraped by with enough to eat.

"A few years of this, and Roy cracked. He waited until Willis had paddled into town in a canoe piled

19

with furs and had been paid for them. Nobody was ever sure what happened next, but suddenly Roy was riding Willis's gray horse and shooting his fancy rifle, and Willis was nowhere to be found.

"When people asked Roy about his neighbor, Roy would tell them, 'He sold me his horse and his gun, and he's trapping farther north.' But some people thought Willis hadn't gone any farther than the bottom of the lake. They had a strong feeling that Roy had killed Willis, sunk his canoe, and left his body for the fish to eat.

"As the months passed, stories started to go around about mysterious blue lights near Willis's cabin. Men traveling after dark said they'd seen a ghostly white canoe, gliding across the waters of the lake. Roy didn't have much of an imagination" — Dr. Beekman winked at me — "so he didn't pay any attention to the stories. But one night, just about midnight, Roy's old dog gave an eerie howl." Dr. Beekman howled, and goosebumps ran down my arms. "Roy woke up with a start and listened, but all was quiet. He'd closed his eyes again, and was about to doze off, when suddenly there was a loud bang at his front door. . . ."

At just that moment, there were three powerful thumps on our front door!

Chapter
3

Patti and Stephanie and I screamed.

Kate jumped about a foot!

"Who could that be?" asked Mrs. Beekman.

"It's Willis!" Melissa yelled.

Dr. Beekman shrugged his shoulders. "If it's Mr. Morrell, he's two days late, but I'm not expecting anyone else." He walked quickly to the door.

I thought I was going to pass out! Patti had ducked under her sleeping bag, so only the end of her nose showed. I saw Kate reach for one of the logs next to the fireplace.

"If a ghost floats across the threshold, I'm going straight out the back door, whether it's open or not!" I whispered breathlessly to Stephanie.

Dr. Beekman grabbed the knob and jerked the door open.

A bright beam of light shone full on his face. "Morris?" a man's voice said. "Is that you?"

"Ira?" said Dr. Beekman. "And Jane? It's the Norwoods."

I let out my breath with a wheeze.

"Did I hear shouts?" Mrs. Norwood asked. "I hope we didn't alarm you."

"Morris was telling the girls a ghost story. Please come in," said Mrs. Beekman. "You already know Kate and Melissa, and these are Kate's friends, Lauren, Patti, and Stephanie. Dr. and Mrs. Norwood."

"Hello, girls. We hadn't seen any lights on in your cabin, and then we noticed the glow of a fire in the windows. We thought we'd make sure you'd gotten here safely," Dr. Norwood explained.

"A lot of the houses are empty at this time of year — there've been break-ins," said Mrs. Norwood. "When we saw a flashlight in back of the cabin — "

"That was me, getting the firewood. Unfortunately, our electricity wasn't turned on. I'll have to take care of it tomorrow. Maybe I could borrow your phone in the morning?" Dr. Beekman said.

"Of course! No electricity?" said Dr. Norwood,

flipping the switch near the door a few times.

"How awful!" Mrs. Norwood said. "Why don't you all bunk with us tonight?"

"Plenty of room," said Dr. Norwood. "Sam and Dave can sleep in the den. . . ."

"Mom!" Kate moaned softly.

"That's very nice of you," Mrs. Beekman said, with a frown at Kate. "But I think we can manage until morning. Thanks so much."

"Then we'll leave you to get some sleep," said Dr. Norwood. "Good night — see you tomorrow."

"Nice people," Dr. Beekman said after he'd closed the door. He glanced at his watch. "It's getting really late. I'd better scoop up some lake water — "

"But, Dr. Beekman," interrupted Stephanie. "You never finished the story!"

I didn't care if we *never* heard the end of the story, but Stephanie and Kate like to get to the bottom of things.

"What happened after the knock on Roy Jonas's door?" Kate asked her father.

Dr. Beekman sat down on the lumpy couch again and took up the story.

" 'Who's there?' Roy Jonas asked shakily. There was no answer, but whoever — or *whatever* — was outside banged on the door so hard that it came off its hinges! Roy found himself face to face with the ghostly spirit of Willis Pyle, complete with the bullet hole Roy had put in him! 'My money!' the ghost demanded. 'What have you done with my money?'

"Roy fainted. When he finally regained consciousness, the sun was rising, and his hair had turned completely white.

"Roy Jonas was never the same. Not long after that, he drowned in the lake. The spirit had gotten its revenge. But people say you can still see Willis paddling his canoe from one shore of the lake to the other, looking for his missing money."

"Oooo!" Melissa huddled closer to her mother.

The hair was standing up on the back of my neck.

"Was the money ever found?" Kate asked.

"No. Roy is supposed to have buried it somewhere, and holes have been dug all over the place, but the money has never turned up," said Dr. Beekman.

"That's enough stories for tonight," said Mrs. Beekman. "Let's get ready for bed, girls."

We ended up dragging two more cots into the biggest bedroom on the second floor and placing them in a circle around the kerosene lantern, kind of like a wagon train in hostile territory.

"Want to play Truth or Dare?" Kate asked. We were all bundled up in our sleeping bags.

"Are you kidding?" Stephanie exclaimed. "Just going outside to the bathroom was as bad as the worst dare I've ever had to do — not to mention washing my face in *brown* lake water!"

"What about your mud facial masks? And just because there was one little spider on the floor of the outdoor toilet . . ." Kate said. Even though she had complained a little herself, she could get defensive if she thought one of us was criticizing her family's choice of location.

"A little spider? It was about the size of a dinner plate!" said Stephanie. "I'm not moving out of this bed until I can see what's coming at me!"

I peered out the window at the lake, which shimmered in the moonlight. If I squinted, I could imagine a silvery canoe was gliding toward us. I closed my eyes tight. "What did you think about that story your father told us, Kate?"

"You know what I think of ghost stories," Kate said. "Silly stuff. The Norwood boys, on the other hand, are all too *real*."

"Whe-e-ere is my monnn-eeey?" Stephanie moaned, imitating Willis.

Patti covered up her head.

"Do you mind?" I said.

"You big chickens!" Kate and Stephanie giggled.

"Oh, yeah? Wait! Listen!" I whispered.

"What?" Stephanie cried.

"Don't you hear it? That scratching noise," I told her. "It's rats in the walls!"

"Eeeee!" Stephanie rolled up into a ball.

"Nyah, nyah — now we're even!" I said to her.

"Okay up there?" Dr. Beekman called from downstairs.

"We're fine," Kate yelled back. "I can tell you one thing — ghosts and rats are nothing compared to Sam and Dave Norwood," she said to us with a big yawn. "Want to play Mad Libs?"

But we were too tired and sleepy to stay awake any longer.

Chapter 4

"There's your father's car," Patti pointed out to Kate.

It was early the next morning. The four of us were behind the Porter house, sitting on a dilapidated pier that stuck out into Spirit Lake.

Dr. Beekman's little red VW was parked across the lake, beside a split-level house with two chimneys and floor-to-ceiling windows facing the water.

"So that's the Norwoods'. I expected something with big iron bars to keep the animals inside," said Kate. "Dad must be calling about the lights."

"It'll be hours before the guy gets here and turns on the electricity so we can take showers," I said. I shredded the last of my breakfast bagel and dropped it into the water for the fish to eat. "Why don't we do something, instead of just hanging around?"

"You probably want to jog for five or ten miles," Stephanie said with a groan. She and Kate tease me about being a jock because I like to run with my brother twice a week.

I stretched and took a deep breath of fresh, piney air. "How about a nice, slow hike along the lake?" I suggested.

"Let's!" said Patti. "It's a beautiful day; there's so much to look at. . . ."

"I could stand to walk off some of this breakfast," Stephanie said, licking cream cheese and jam off her finger, "before it collects on my hips."

"All right." Kate got to her feet. "As long as we stay away from *them*." She waved toward the Norwoods'.

"No problem. We'll just go in the opposite direction," I said.

We headed off, walking on the pebbles that lined the edge of the lake. Spirit Lake was pretty, with lots of ducks and swans and huge clumps of water lilies. The houses built on it were all different styles, from real log cabins to super-modern, to a small stone house that looked like it was right out of a fairy tale.

The pebbles on the shore of the lake were slippery and not so easy to walk on. As the sun rose higher in the sky, we started to get warm. Stephanie's cheeks were turning pink.

"I don't know about you," she said, "but I'm roasting." She took off her sweater and plopped down on a flat rock. "Even my feet are hot!" Stephanie pulled off her shoes and socks. Then she stuck her toes in the water.

"Cold!" she squealed. But she lowered her feet all the way in. "It feels good."

I took off my sneakers, too, and rolled up my jeans. I waded into the lake up to my calves. The water was freezing at first, but I got used to it.

It was really peaceful there. A family of turtles was sunning itself on the trunk of a dead pine that had fallen into the water. A couple of geese were diving for weeds not far away. Minnows nibbled at my ankles. "This is nice!" I said to Kate and Patti.

"Maybe I can catch one of those turtles for Horace," Patti said, peeling off her sneakers. Unlike a lot of people I know, Patti sincerely likes her brother. It's partly because Patti is an unusually patient person, but also because Horace is all right, for a first-grader who happens to be incredibly intelligent. "The lizard I bought him in the city got away last week. A turtle would cheer him up."

She was rolling up her sweats when Kate murmured, "Red alert — here they come!" She looked wildly around. "We can hide in those trees until they go away. . . ." Whirling, she trotted toward a grove of maples.

"Is it the Norwoods?" Patti asked.

Two boys in orange life jackets were paddling a yellow inflatable boat in our direction.

"Who else?" Kate called over her shoulder. "Hurry!"

"But they've already seen us!" I said.

The boys waved and shouted: "Hello-o-o!"

"They seem friendly enough." I waved back.

"And it's rocky up there — we don't have our shoes on!" Stephanie complained. She was studying the boys as they got nearer. "Besides, they're just little kids. How bad could they be?"

"Ha! You'd have to be an only child to say that and mean it!" Kate told Stephanie, who *is* an only child. But she walked slowly back down the slope.

The boys stopped paddling when they were about thirty feet away and let their rubber boat drift toward shore. They were both skinny, with narrow heads and haircuts that were too short for their ears, which stuck out. The larger boy was wearing dark glasses.

"Hey, Kate," he said. He looked about nine.

"Hey, Sam," Kate said, keeping her distance from the lake and the Norwoods.

"Hi," said the smaller one, who had to be Dave by process of elimination.

"Hi," Stephanie and Patti and I said. Were these the monsters Kate had told us about?

"Mom wanted us to invite you girls to our house for early dinner," said Sam.

"I'm sure we can't. My mother has something else planned," Kate said cagily.

"No, she doesn't," said Dave. He had kind of a raspy voice and buck teeth. "She already said yes."

Kate rolled her eyes. "Wonderful! What time?"

"Around four-thirty," Sam said. "It's a barbe-cue."

"What are you doing?" Dave was watching Patti, who was wading cautiously closer to the turtles on the tree trunk.

"I'd like to catch one of those turtles for my little brother," she answered. "But I can't tell how deep the water is."

"Oh, that's easy," said Sam. He paddled the boat forward until he was about the same distance from shore as the sleeping turtles were. "This lake is shallow for a long way out."

"Don't believe him!" Kate warned us.

But at the same time Sam was proving to us that the lake *was* shallow. Lowering his paddle into the water, he said, "I'm touching bottom with the paddle right now." He pulled it out to show us the depth. "See? It's not much over your knees."

"Thanks, very much," said Patti. "Lauren, can you help me? I'll walk on this side of the trunk, and you walk on the other. . . ."

Sam and Dave drifted up closer to me, eager not to miss anything. The turtles hadn't moved at all. Their eyes were shut, their necks stretched out to soak up the sun.

"Slowly," Patti warned me. "I don't want to scare them."

We took a step, then another and suddenly we were up to our noses in icy cold water! The bottom of the lake had dropped from less than a foot to about four feet!

My ears were full of water, but I could still hear Sam and Dave Norwood screaming with laughter. I wanted to strangle them! Or at least dump them into the lake. Shaking with cold — or maybe it was anger — I lunged for their boat.

"Hey, you'll get us wet!" Dave shrieked as I hooked my arm over the top.

"Yeah, watch it!" Sam whacked at me with his plastic paddle, but not before I'd managed to jerk open the valve on the side of the boat where you fill it with air. I turned my back on the Norwood brothers and staggered out of the lake.

"Way to go, Lauren!" Kate yelled.

By the time I got to shore, the boat was starting to wilt. Sam and Dave were paddling like maniacs, but they didn't quite make it. The rubber boat folded in the middle and set them down in about a foot of water, which is deep enough to get you pretty damp if you're sitting down.

"You'll be sorry!" Dave howled. He was so mad he was smacking the water with his paddle and splashing himself and his brother.

Stephanie was helping Patti out of the lake. Patti's teeth were chattering, her lips were blue, and her sweats had soaked up water like a sponge.

"A couple of terrific kids, aren't they?" Kate observed as the boys dragged their deflated boat to shore. "Come on. We'd better get back before you both catch pneumonia!"

When we sloshed into the Porter house, Mrs. Beekman was sweeping some of the cobwebs out of the living room. "Lauren! Patti!" she exclaimed. "What in the world happened to you?"

Melissa giggled. "You look funny!"

"Those creepy Norwood boys ambushed us!" Kate ignored Melissa and glared at her mother. "How could you say that we'd go to dinner at their house?"

"What else could I do, Kate?" Mrs. Beekman replied, digging through bags and boxes for some clean towels for us. "Dr. Norwood works with Daddy, and I couldn't be rude. It's just for a few hours. . . ."

"They did this in *five minutes!*" Kate said, pointing to Patti and me. "I hate to think what they might do in a few hours!"

Mrs. Beekman shook her head and sighed. "Lauren, you and Patti change out of those wet clothes, then come warm up by the fire. I'm glad we didn't let it go out. . . ."

Patti and I had finished toweling dry and dressing again when we heard Dr. Beekman's voice. "We're finished in the cellar," he was saying to Mrs. Beekman. "Let's try the lights."

"They work!" Melissa yelled. "I can plug in my Lite-Brite!"

"Ice cubes and showers!" said Kate.

"No more outdoor toilet!" Stephanie added.

I pushed up the switch in our bedroom, and the

lamp in the corner blinked on. "No more dark nights," I told Patti.

When we got downstairs, Dr. Beekman was paying a man who had bushy black eyebrows and a toothy smile.

The man stuck the bills in his jacket pocket. "Like I said, I can't guarantee how long the lights'll *stay* on — these wires are old and worn. All it takes is a mouse running across 'em . . . or a ghost . . . and we happen to have a few of them around here." He kind of leered at all of us. "Yeah — if I was you, I wouldn't wander around after dark. Never know what you're going to run into."

The man nodded at Dr. Beekman. Then he sauntered down the front steps and climbed into an old green van.

"Mr. Morrell?" Patti asked.

"Right. Apparently the electricity was on all along, but one of the main lines from the fuse box had frayed, so it wasn't feeding up to the house," Dr. Beekman told us.

"What did Mr. Morrell mean about ghosts?" I wanted to know.

"Oh, I think he enjoys needling the vacationers," Dr. Beekman said. "I wouldn't pay any attention."

Chapter 5

After we'd had lunch, and then showered and washed and dried our hair, it was time to go to the Norwoods'. Since their house wasn't far away, we all squeezed into Mrs. Beekman's car. Melissa sat in the front seat with Dr. and Mrs. Beekman, and Kate, Stephanie, Patti, and I stuffed into the back.

"We're going right into the heart of enemy territory," Kate murmured to the three of us. "So there are a few things to remember. Rule One: Don't let Sam and Dave get too close to you; Rule Two: Don't take anything from them; Rule Three: Never turn your back on them; and Rule Four: Never believe a thing they say. With luck, that should get us safely through dinner."

"You make them sound like Public Enemy Number One!" said Stephanie. "They're not that smart. They played a dumb trick that Lauren and Patti happened to fall for." She tried to hide a grin. "You looked pretty silly: Now you see 'em, now you don't."

"How funny is it going to be when they get *you?*" I asked.

"They're not going to get me," said Stephanie breezily. "Carter Poole, this little kid who lived down the hall in our apartment building in the city, tried every practical joke in the book on me, and never got me once! I'm immune."

Sam and Dave were waiting on the front steps with their father, hair slicked down, shirts tucked in, expressions pleasant, when we drove up to the Norwoods' house. The boys smiled brightly as we got out of the car.

"Welcome, welcome," Dr. Norwood said. "I think you've all met Sam and Dave. . . ."

The four of us nodded, watching them warily.

"Why don't I show you around first? Then we'll go out back, where Jane's firing up the barbecue," said Dr. Norwood. "This is the living room." He led us into a long, high-ceilinged room with lots of photographs on the walls. "Jane's the photographer in the family."

While we were checking out Mrs. Norwood's

photos of the lake at different times of the year, Sam sidled up to me. "Sorry about this morning, Lauren. Shake," he said, sticking his hand out.

"Don't, Lauren," Stephanie warned me. "I bet he's got one of those buzzers that shocks you when your hand touches his."

I stuck my hands in my pocket. Sam scowled at Stephanie.

"Give it to me," Dr. Norwood said to his oldest son.

"What, Dad?" Sam said, trying to look innocent.

"The joy buzzer you've got in your hand," said Dr. Norwood. "Right now!"

"Aw, Dad!" But Sam handed it over.

"Boys will be boys, I guess," Dr. Norwood said to us.

"Yeah, and now they're armed," Kate hissed.

"The dining room is in here." Dr. Norwood went on with the tour. The walls were covered with shelves of books. "Didn't I hear Barbara say something about your telling the girls ghost stories, Morris?" He reached for a small blue paperback. "This might interest you: It's about ghosts seen in this area."

The name of the book was *Famous Wraiths of Sussex County*. Under the title there was a drawing

of a transparent woman in a long white gown, crook-
ing her finger.

Dr. Norwood opened the book and flipped
through it quickly. "In fact," he said, "once there
was a ghost associated with Charlie Porter's house,
when it belonged to some people named Miller."

I drew in my breath with a gasp. "Willis Pyle?"
I barely managed to squeak.

Dr. Norwood shook his head. "No. Roy Jonas's
cabin was on this side of the lake, about three hundred
feet from our property line, as a matter of fact." He
pointed to the left. "So Willis's ghost sticks to our
neighborhood. The ghost at your house" — he flipped
through the pages — "I'll read you what the author
says: 'It's one of the most delightful hauntings ever
. . . the running footsteps and lilting laughter of a
small child . . . halting musical notes, repeated over
and over again, as if a child were practicing on a
wooden flute. . . .'"

Sam and Dave had been pinching and shoving
each other, but now they were all ears.

"May I see the book, Dr. Norwood?" Kate asked.

"Surely." Dr. Norwood handed it to her. "Morris, Barbara, the den is in here, along with the bedrooms." We stepped down to the lower level of the

house and into the den. The Norwoods had a huge TV set.

"It says that once there was a snowstorm in the summertime — inside someone's house!" Kate was leafing through the book and chuckling to herself.

"Don't you believe in ghosts?" said Sam.

"Give me a break!" Kate replied.

"Patti, how about some lemon drops?" Dave offered her a frosted-glass jar.

"Don't mind if I do," said Stephanie, intercepting the jar. She held it away from her as she unscrewed the top. Two green paper snakes sprang out of it on springs, shooting straight into Dave's face. "Ho-hum," said Stephanie.

"Think you're so smart!" Dave was turning beet-red, gearing up for a tantrum like the one he'd had that morning on the lake.

Dr. Norwood looked at Stephanie with approval. "You're good — you wouldn't want to baby-sit for us sometime, would you? We pay twice as much as anybody else."

I wouldn't baby-sit Sam and Dave Norwood for twenty-five dollars an hour!

"Um, I don't do much baby-sitting," Stephanie said.

"So far, the score for the afternoon is Sleepover

Friends — two, Norwood brothers — zip!" Kate said just loud enough for Sam and Dave to hear.

Sam stuck out his tongue and made a rude noise.

"This is the family room." Dr. Norwood led us to a room at the back of the house, with the floor-to-ceiling windows we could see from Dr. Porter's cabin. He pushed open the sliding doors so we could step out onto the deck. "And here's Jane."

Mrs. Norwood was standing next to a big round grill, a long fork in her hand. "Hi, everybody," she said. "We're having roast loin of pork for dinner" — it smelled fantastic — "but it'll be a while before it's done. If anyone wants a snack to stave off hunger pangs in the meantime, just yell. We can use the microwave to heat up some Italian sausages I grilled at lunch."

"Want to try your luck at fishing?" Dr. Norwood asked us. "We've got four poles. . . ."

"Two of 'em are mine and Sam's!" Dave whined, grabbing one of the cane fishing poles lying on the Norwoods' deck.

"David!" Dr. Norwood said sternly. "We share with our guests!"

Stephanie smiled sweetly at Dave as she took his pole. "Thanks so much," she said. "What are we using for bait? Bacon?"

"Worms!" Sam Norwood replied gleefully. He poked an old paint can under Stephanie's nose. "What do you like? Red wrigglers or nightcrawlers?"

"Eeeeugh!" Stephanie screeched, backing up fast. Sam came after her with the can.

"Stop that!" thundered Dr. Norwood.

I took the worms away from Sam. The can was absolutely squirming with them, a big ball of pinkish-red earthworms.

Stephanie shuddered. "I can't stand worms," she admitted. She handed the fishing pole she was holding to Melissa. "You fish — I'll watch."

We walked out to the dock, where Dr. Norwood baited our hooks for us. Melissa, Kate, Patti, and I dropped the lines in the water, and waited for the red-and-white floats to bob.

Patti was the first to get a bite. "It's moving!" she whispered, wide-eyed, as her float jumped up and down.

"Wait a second . . . let the fish take the hook," Dr. Norwood advised. "Okay . . . steady . . . jerk it out!"

Patti doesn't know her own strength. She jerked so hard that the little yellow fish on the other end of the line sailed into the air, and the hook fell out of its mouth. The fish hit the lake with a slap and scooted away from the dock.

Sam and Dave snickered. "Dumb girls!" Dave muttered.

"Never mind, you've got the idea," Dr. Norwood told Patti. "Try again." Kate's dad baited Patti's hook with a fat nightcrawler, and she dropped it back into the water.

I caught a small perch, like the one that had gotten away from Patti, and Kate caught a baby trout. We didn't keep them — Dr. Norwood took the hooks out of their mouths and dropped the fish back into the lake.

While we fished, Stephanie read to us from *Famous Wraiths*: "Did you know ghosts are specialized? Indoor ghosts stay indoors, and outdoor ghosts outdoors. At one house, there was even a ghost dog!"

"Indoor or outdoor?" Kate asked with a giggle.

Melissa hooked the biggest fish, a white bass that really fought. Kate and I helped her pull it out, and Dr. Beekman turned it loose. About then I announced, "I'm hungry — I can't help it." It had been a while since lunch, and Mrs. Norwood was still basting the pork loin.

"Me, too," Stephanie said, standing up and sticking the book into her pocket. "I'll get us some sausages."

"The boys will do it," Dr. Norwood told her.

"Anybody else want sausages besides Lauren and Stephanie? No? Sam, bring some sausages on two rolls, please."

"I'd like mustard on mine, please," Stephanie said to Sam.

Sam glowered at her, but soon he was back with two sandwiches on a plate. Stephanie took one, I took the other.

I was about to bite into mine when I remembered Rule Two: Don't take anything from them. I looked up just in time to catch Sam nudging his little brother. The sandwich was awfully flat . . . "Stephanie, don't!" I shouted.

Too late. Stephanie had already taken a bite out of the end of her roll. But she didn't chew it or swallow it. Instead, she dug it out of her mouth and pulled it apart. "Okay, here," she said. "No sausage, though."

I had an awful feeling. . . . I laid my pole down on the dock and opened the two halves of the roll I was holding. Inside, covered with mustard, lay an enormous red wriggler! And when Stephanie checked out the rest of her roll, they probably heard her scream back in Riverhurst!

Chapter 6

Stephanie yelled so loud that she startled Sam and Dave, at least. They took off, around the house, with Dr. Norwood hot on their trail.

Somebody was going to have to hang around to appreciate Mrs. Norwood's cooking, but it wasn't going to be us. After a close call with a worm sandwich, not even *I* could think about dinner.

"Morris, why don't you drive the girls back to the cabin?" Mrs. Beekman said with one quick look at Stephanie's greenish face. "Melissa and I will wait here."

"Let me cut some pork loin to take with you," Mrs. Norwood urged as Kate, Patti, Stephanie, and I climbed into the car. "It's ready now. Please?" She was practically wringing her hands.

Pink meat wasn't tops on my list of attractive foods just then, and pork loin was definitely pink. "Uh . . . I don't think we're very hungry, Mrs. Norwood. Thanks, anyway," I said, swallowing hard.

Stephanie couldn't even manage to answer. "I think I'm going to be sick," she groaned over and over. But we made it to the cabin safely.

"Can we bring you some leftovers at least? Cole slaw? Potato salad?" Dr. Beekman asked before he drove back to the Norwoods'.

"If we get hungry, we can stir something up here, Daddy," Kate told him. "Mom packed enough stuff to last for two weeks."

"Keep the door locked," said Dr. Beekman. "We won't stay late. And if you need us, shine a flashlight in our direction — I'll be here right away."

"We'll be fine," Kate said, as Stephanie crawled upstairs to the bathroom.

I was right behind her. "That is without a doubt the grossest thing that's ever happened to me in my whole life!" she moaned. *"Yech!"* Stephanie took an enormous swig of mouthwash and gargled loudly.

I squirted toothpaste onto my toothbrush and worked up a lather. "We were lucky that earthworms curl up when they're scared," I said through the foam.

"Otherwise, we would've bitten their" — I gulped — "their heads off!"

"Gag me with a stick!" Stephanie muttered. "I could cheerfully murder those little monsters! And what punishment will they get for trying to feed us worms? Probably sent to bed — big deal!"

I was giving my mouth one last swipe with the toothbrush when I heard Kate exclaim from the living room: "Patti . . . it's a secret cubbyhole!"

We hurried downstairs to find Patti holding a small leather pouch wrapped with brown cord. There was a square hole in the side of the fireplace behind her; a brick lay on the floor underneath it.

Patti weighed the pouch in her hand. "It's heavy," she said.

"Untie it!" Stephanie said.

Patti tugged at the knots without budging them. "I'll cut it with our bread knife," said Kate, taking the pouch.

A few slices, and the string fell away. The mouth of the pouch opened, and Kate poured whatever was inside into her hand.

"What is it?" I asked as we crowded closer.

"Old coins," Kate said.

"Maybe Dr. Norwood was wrong," I said slowly.

The hairs stood up on the back of my neck. "Maybe it's Willis Pyle's long-lost money!"

"Are there dates on the coins?" Stephanie asked Kate.

Kate gave each of us two or three coins to examine.

"They're gold!" The coins in my hand were beautiful: One had a woman's head with a feather crown on it, another an eagle with a shield on its chest. I held them under the lamp next to the couch. "I've got a three-dollar gold piece from 1877, a ten-dollar one from 1880, and a five-dollar one from 1878," I said.

"Mine are from around the same time," said Kate. "1879, and two from 1881."

"Mine, too," Stephanie said. "So it couldn't have been Willis Pyle's money. He died in 1853, according to this book, and Roy Jonas died two years later." She pulled the book out of her pocket. "I forgot to return it to Dr. Norwood in all the excitement."

"What about the child ghost?" Patti asked.

"According to the writer, nobody knows who that ghost belongs to," Stephanie said. "It popped up about seventy years ago, when this house was owned by somebody named Donald Miller. His wife heard the ghost running around upstairs and giggling.

It sang to their little daughter, and Mr. Miller heard it playing the flute once or twice. How did you ever find the pouch?'' she asked Patti.

Patti shoved the brick back into the hole in the fireplace. "I leaned against this brick with my hand when I was laying another log on the fire,'' she said. "It felt kind of loose, so I jiggled it'' — she moved the brick back and forth to show me — "and pulled it out. The leather pouch had been jammed in behind it.''

"It's about the right height for a child's hiding-place,'' I said thoughtfully.

"What child would have had so much money?'' Kate checked her coins. "I have two fives, a three, and a ten — twenty-three dollars.''

"I have eighteen,'' I said, adding up my coins.

"There's twenty-two dollars here.'' Patty counted her coins back into the pouch.

"Stephanie?'' Kate said.

"Sixteen . . . but they're solid gold and more than a hundred years old! They're probably worth twenty times that! Are you kidding me? We're rich!''

"*Dr. Porter's* rich,'' Patti corrected Stephanie. She collected the coins from us and stuck the pouch of money behind the brick again, for safekeeping.

"Well, what about a reward?'' said Stephanie.

"Maybe there's more gold — this house could be stuffed with it!"

She and Kate and Patti and I started jiggling each brick in the fireplace. We got pretty dusty, but we didn't find anymore treasures.

"What about the walls?" Kate suggested. "Lots of times, old houses had secret passages. . . ." She knocked on the living room wall next to the door and was rewarded with a shower of plaster.

"Look, it's snowing inside the house!" Stephanie giggled. "It must be the ghost!"

We tapped all over the walls of the cabin, until Kate announced she was hungry.

"What's there to eat?" I asked. The money had taken my mind off the worm just long enough for my stomach to start acting normal again.

"I'll go through Mom's supplies," Kate said.

"Will Dr. Porter mind if we raid his kitchen for extra ingredients?"

Kate shook her head. "Dad can pay him back. You guys look in the cabinets."

Dr. Porter's cupboard was not exactly crowded with food, but what he had was interesting: some jars of shrimp cocktail, a container of smoked cheese spread, a metal box of fancy crackers, six small bottles of jam made from fruits I'd never heard of, like "scuppernongs," and "maypops."

"Why don't we each make something?" Patti said. She hunted through Mrs. Beekman's collection of bags and boxes, too, and came up with a large can of tunafish, a package of English muffins, and some Velveeta cheese. "I'll do tuna melts."

"I'm going to make sloppy joes," said Kate, dumping a can of chili into a pan to heat it up.

"I'll be in charge of appetizers," I told them. That was easy: shrimp cocktails or smoked cheese spread on crackers.

"I guess that leaves dessert to me," Stephanie said. She stood on a chair to ransack Dr. Porter's cabinets, taking down the jams and a box of biscuit mix.

We messed up a lot of dishes. After all, there was a dishwasher we could use later, Dr. Porter's single luxury. But dinner was good. Even Stephanie's dessert worked out okay: hot biscuits stuffed with jam.

It had gotten dark while we were eating. We could look across the lake and see the lights on in the Norwoods' house.

"I'm going to get those brats before we leave," Stephanie said, eyes narrowed. "I definitely owe them one."

"We'll think of something," Kate said. "What should we do now?"

"No TV, no phone, not even a radio," Stephanie said listlessly. For lack of anything better to do, she ate another piece of tuna melt.

I was full, kind of sleepy, and my mind was wandering back to the hidden gold. "Maybe the child's parents caught some awful disease, the way people did in those days, and as they lay in their beds, wasting away, they asked him — or her — to hide their life savings," I thought out loud. "So the child hid the pouch in the fireplace, and then got sick himself, and died, too. . . ."

"Maybe the kid was a bank robber." Kate thinks it's her duty to bring me down to earth sometimes.

I frowned at her. "It'll be a mystery forever," I said.

Stephanie had perked up. "I know a way we could find out!"

"How?" Patti asked a little nervously. Sometimes it's hard to guess *what* Stephanie's going to come up with.

"Have a séance!" Stephanie replied.

"A say-ahnce?" I repeated.

"You know, sit around a table and call up the ghost!"

Chapter 7

"Séance" is a word I'd read, but never heard spoken, which is why I didn't recognize it; I thought you said it "seence." I knew one thing for sure — I didn't want to have one in that spooky old house!

"Uh, do you think that's such a good idea?" Patti asked cautiously.

"Call up a ghost?" Kate chortled. "Get real, Stephanie!"

"Oh, not that I think it'd *really* work," Stephanie said quickly. She didn't want Kate to accuse *her* of letting her imagination run wild. "But we don't have anything better to do, do we?"

"What if — a chance in a million, I know — it does work?" I asked.

"We're talking about a nice ghost, remember?" Stephanie tapped the little blue book of *Famous Wraiths* she'd left lying on the table. " 'Runs, laughs, plays a flute?' What have we got to lose? Come on, it'll be fun!"

"I suppose you know all about conducting a séance," Kate said, raising an eyebrow at Stephanie.

"I saw a play once in the city . . ."

Kate groaned and rolled her eyes. "In the city, naturally!"

". . . that told all about séances!" Stephanie tossed her head as if to say, So there! "Let's clear everything off the table."

"Now what?" Kate asked after we'd piled the dirty dishes in the sink.

"The first step is to breathe some fresh air." Stephanie slid the living room windows up. "Take a deep breath," she instructed.

"What's that supposed to accomplish?" Kate asked.

"It clears your mind," Stephanie replied. "Breathe!"

We all breathed in with a gasp.

"Now another one," Stephanie said.

"Can we breathe out first?" Kate rasped, still holding her first breath.

"Very funny!" said Stephanie crossly. "Of course you breathe out after you breathe in!"

We huffed and puffed at the windows for a minute or two. Then Stephanie told us to sit down at the table. "Two on each side," she said, sliding into the chair next to mine. She and I were on one side of the table, and Patti and Kate were directly across from us.

"What about turning the lights off?" asked Kate. "I thought séances were always held in the dark."

"I'm trying to get us settled first. Place your hands flat on the table, close enough to touch fingers with the people on either side of you."

I put my hands on the table, palms down. On the left my little finger touched Stephanie's, and across the table on my right, Patti's.

"I guess this is to make sure no one cheats," Kate said.

"What do you mean, 'cheats?' " I asked.

"Like knocking on the table and pretending it's a ghost who's doing it," Kate said.

"That's right." Stephanie pushed her chair back. "Okay, I'm turning off the lights."

She walked to the switch near the front door and clicked it off. Thank goodness for the fire burning in the fireplace, or the room would have been pitch-black!

Stephanie sat down again. "Touch fingers . . . now we need some music."

"Where are we going to get music?" said Kate. "No TV, no radio, remember?"

"Then we'll just have to sing," Stephanie replied.

"Sing?" Kate doesn't have a very good voice, so she hates to sing out loud. "Sing what?"

"Oh, something a kid would like. We're trying to attract a child, aren't we?" Stephanie said blithely. "I know: 'She'll Be Comin' 'Round the Mountain.'"

There was something very creepy about sitting in the dark, singing for a child's ghost, even if I didn't *really* believe in such things.

Patti sounded as quavery as I felt: "She'll b-be comin' 'round the m-mountain when she c-comes. . . ."

We sang a couple of verses, until Stephanie said, "That should be enough. Now we have to concentrate on nothing."

"How do you concentrate on nothing?" I wanted to know. It seemed to me that concentrating on *nothing* was concentrating on *something*.

"Just empty your mind completely," Stephanie directed.

I had a hard time with that one, because my

eyes kept wandering into the darkest corners of the room, half-expecting to see a small, transparent shape. . . .

"Okay, here goes," Stephanie announced in a low voice. "Is there anyone here?"

I felt very queasy. Maybe I shouldn't have eaten that last sloppy joe.

Across from me, Kate started snickering.

"Are you going to be serious, or not?" Stephanie hissed. Then she repeated, "Is there anyone here? One knock for yes . . . two knocks for no."

We all sat absolutely still, hardly breathing.

"One knock for yes," Stephanie whispered again.

I was so tense that my leg suddenly cramped. My foot went sideways, crashing against the base of the table — I couldn't control it.

Everyone yelped and jumped a mile — even Kate.

"That was me," I admitted.

"Lauren!" Stephanie scolded.

"Sorry, just a cramp in my calf," I explained, leaning down to massage it.

"Concentrate!" Stephanie ordered. "Is anybody here? We'd just like to talk to you . . . one knock for yes. . . ."

We waited in the dark for what seemed like hours, until Kate finally spoke up. "This is dumb!"

she said, sliding her chair back. "I'm turning on the light."

But before she could stand up, there was a loud bang!

"Did any of you do that?" Kate whispered.

"N-no!" Patti and I stuttered.

"It sounded like it was coming from across the room," Stephanie whispered back. "Near the windows."

"It was the broom," Kate said. "Mom leaned the broom against the wall next to a window. The wind must have blown it over."

"Unh-uh, it wasn't the broom, Kate. I can s-see it, still standing up," I whispered.

"Then a dead branch fell off a tree outside," Kate insisted. "I'll take a look. . . ."

"Wait a minute!" Stephanie hissed. "What if we've really got something?"

I heard somebody moan softly. It took me a while to figure out *I* was doing it!"

"Are you a girl, or a boy? Knock once for a girl, and twice for a boy." Stephanie spoke into the darkness.

For a few seconds, all was quiet. But just when I was deciding the whole thing was a fluke, that Kate was right, there were two loud bangs!

"I c-can't b-believe this!" Patti squeaked.

"Sssh!" Stephanie said. "You'll scare him!" She talked to the ghost again. "How old are you? Knock once if you're under ten years old, and twice if you're over ten."

Bang!

"There has to be some explanation!" Kate said through clenched teeth. She started to stand up.

"Sit down!" Stephanie ordered sharply in a whisper. "What year did you . . . uh . . . die?" she asked the ghost. "Knock once if I've said the right year . . . 1881" — that was the last date on the gold coins Patti had found.

Stephanie waited, but there wasn't a sound. "1882?" she said.

Silence.

"1883," said Stephanie.

A *bang!* near the windows.

I could feel Patti's fingers shaking, and Stephanie's felt pretty shivery, too. We were actually having a conversation with a little boy who died in 1883 before he was ten years old!

That's when we heard someone giggle.

"I knew it!" Kate exploded, pushing her chair back and racing toward the windows. "It's those disgusting Norwoods!"

Chapter
8

"Just wait till I catch you!" Kate roared. She didn't bother with the front door. She practically dove through an open window. We could hear her crashing through the tall weeds outside. Then there was a sharp *clang* followed by a louder groan!

"Did they get her?" Stephanie exclaimed, meaning the Norwoods. She and Patti and I dashed to the window and peered into the murky front yard.

"Kate, where are you?" I yelled.

"Are you all right?" Patti called out.

"I'm fine!" We saw her scramble to her feet. "I fell over an old bucket." She gave it an angry kick. "Come on!"

Kate sped across Dr. Porter's yard and around the house toward the lake.

We didn't have time to look for flashlights or even unlock the front door. Stephanie, Patti, and I tumbled through the open window, too.

The moon was shining, but not enough to help us through the obstacle course of weeds and stumps and bushes outside the cabin. Patti tripped twice, and I stepped on the end of an old rake and just missed bashing my head with the handle.

"Where'd Kate go?" Stephanie was already panting; she's too short-legged to be much of a runner.

"I think that's her white sweatshirt, to the right of the dock," I answered, putting on more speed.

I caught up with Kate at the edge of Spirit Lake. "Do you see them?" I asked her. I was remembering how interested the Norwood boys had been in the ghost story, and how Sam had asked Kate if she believed in ghosts, and I was getting angrier and angrier — those little creeps!

"No, I figured they sneaked out of their house and rowed across," Kate replied.

"No sign of a boat," I said, squinting at the shimmering water.

"Then they're probably taking the shortest way home on foot — right along the shore," Kate said. "Let's get 'em!"

At least there was nothing to fall over at the edge of the lake. We crunched along on the pebbles as fast as we could, past a white wooden cabin and a low house with a flat roof, and a gray stone cottage. There wasn't a light on anywhere. There weren't any Norwoods in sight, either.

Kate stopped for a second to catch her breath, sinking down on an old piling. That's when Stephanie and Patti caught up with us.

"How far ahead of us are they?" Stephanie barely managed to wheeze.

"We haven't really caught sight of them yet," I had to admit.

"That far, huh?" Stephanie plopped down on the piling next to Kate's.

"Do you think they can run that fast?" Patti asked doubtfully. "Dave especially is pretty short. . . ."

"So where are they?" Stephanie asked her.

"Maybe they're hiding," Patti suggested. "With no one in any of these houses, there are plenty of places to hide — under porches, behind garages. . . ."

"If that's the case, we'll never find them," I said.

"Not without flashlights," Stephanie pointed out.

Kate nodded. "Two of us should stay here, just in case Sam and Dave decide to break cover. The other two can go for the flashlights: you and Stephanie, Patti."

"Okay," Patti agreed.

"No way. I'm exhausted!" Stephanie argued. "I can't run another inch. Why don't Patti and Lauren go? They're taller than we are, and faster."

"She's right," I said. "Let's go, Patti."

"Hold it!" Kate whispered. "I think I just heard something!"

All four of us froze. There was the sound of water lapping against the pebbles, and a soft breeze blowing through the pines and rustling the dry leaves on the ground.

"I don't hear anything," Stephanie said at last.

"Yes, there it is again!" Kate hissed. "It's kind of a scraping noise."

"I hear it, too," Patti murmured. "I think it's coming from outside that big two-story." The house was dark. Wooden shutters covered the windows.

"So that's where they're hiding!" Kate gloated. "Are they ever in for a surprise!"

She darted around the hedge at the bottom of the yard, and crept across the sloping lawn. Patti and Stephanie and I were right behind her.

The scraping noise was loud enough for me to hear this time — it sounded like something being dragged. Kate led us up to the back of the big shingled house and started around the side. Suddenly, she stopped dead in her tracks.

I wasn't ready for it. I bumped right into Kate, and Stephanie into me. We started to giggle, but Kate slapped her hands over our mouths.

"Quiet!" she whispered so faintly I could barely understand her. "It's burglars!"

Patti gasped, then covered her own mouth.

I swallowed hard. First ghosts, then Norwoods, then burglars — which was it?

Kate motioned us away from the house to crouch down behind an azalea bush.

"Burglars?" Patti said anxiously.

"Mrs. Norwood mentioned something about lots of break-ins around here," I remembered.

"Are you positive?" Stephanie asked Kate.

"Why else would two guys be dragging furniture out of a house at night with no lights on?" Kate answered.

"Maybe they're moving, and their electricity is off," Stephanie suggested. "Ours was."

"Why don't *you* take a look!" Kate said.

All four of us sneaked across the lawn again. We peered around the corner of the house. Sitting in the driveway like a huge black box was a dark-colored van with the side panels opened wide.

"I don't see anybody," Stephanie whispered.

"Shhh! Just wait a second!" Kate told her.

There was a thump inside the house. Then a screen door creaked open not twenty feet from where we were standing. A heavy-set man backed through the doorway and onto the stoop. He was carrying one end of a chest of drawers. It was heavy, and he kind of grunted as he took the steps one at a time.

"I'm going to break my back with this one!" he complained to the man carrying the other end.

"Quit griping!" the second man snarled. "It's old—we can get a lot of money for this junk!"

As they maneuvered down the rest of the steps and out of the shadow of the house, the moonlight shone on their faces for a split second.

"Kate! It's — " I whispered in her ear.

She nodded and waved us back toward the azalea bush. When we were all safely hidden behind it, Kate finished my sentence for me: "Mr. Morrell!"

"You're kidding!" Stephanie said.

I shook my head. "He's got on the same plaid shirt he was wearing this morning, and that must be his van parked in the driveway. It's dark green, which looks black at night."

"No wonder Morrell told us to stay inside at

night," said Kate. "Ghosts had nothing to do with it."

"It's perfect!" said Stephanie. "He's probably been in most of the houses around here, fixing wiring, turning the water on or off. . . ."

"Right — and while he's working, he can check the place out for antiques or whatever, without calling any attention to himself," I said. "He knows exactly what he'll steal from each house before he breaks in."

"*If* he breaks in," Kate said. "Since he's kind of a caretaker, he probably has keys to some of the cottages. It's all very neat, isn't it?"

"So what are we going to do?" I asked her.

"We have to get help," Patti said.

"If only we had a phone!" said Stephanie.

"We could run to the Norwoods' house," I said.

"Too far," said Kate. "By the time we got there, Morrell would be long gone." She was quiet for a moment. "Maybe the best thing would be to try to signal Dad with a flashlight from Dr. Porter's cabin." She looked at me. "You go, Lauren, and Patti."

"What about you and Stephanie?" I asked her.

"Yeah, what about us?" Stephanie said nervously.

"We'll stay here — keep an eye on those guys."

"But . . ." I started to argue. "What if . . . What if Kate and Stephanie were spotted?"

"Go on!" Kate ordered. "No one's going to see us under this azalea. Don't waste any more time!"

Patti and I crept down the lawn, past the hedge, to the lake. Then we sprinted to Dr. Porter's house along the shore.

I don't think I've ever run faster in my life, or Patti, either. We made it to his decrepit old dock in a few minutes and dashed through the weeds to the back door of the house.

"Locked!" I said after I'd tried the handle.

"We came out the front!" Patti reminded me. She raced around the house.

But the front door was locked, too. We'd crawled out the window, of course! Patti's lighter than I am, so I gave her a leg up. She wriggled through the window and dropped with a thud on the other side. "Patti, don't turn on the lights!" I warned. "Morrell might see them and make a run for it!"

Patti darted to the front door and slid back the bolt so I could get in. Then we grabbed the first flashlight we could find. Luckily, Dr. Beekman's was on the mantel, where he'd left it after his trip to the cellar with *Mr. Morrell* that morning.

I ran out the back door with the flashlight. "Which

is the Norwood house?" I asked Patti. There were several houses with lights on across the lake, and everything looked so different at night.

"The long one with the yellow lantern at the end of the dock," Patti told me.

"I'm sure they're all inside now — I hope they remember to glance over here once in a while." I turned the flashlight on and shone it toward the Norwoods'. I clicked it off and on, on and off.

"What about an SOS?" Patti said.

"Good idea." I blinked three short flashes, three long ones, three short ones. I did it again and again, until my finger went numb.

"They haven't given us a thought," I groaned. "They're sitting around, talking, and digesting pork loin."

"Wait a second — look!" said Patti.

At the side of the long house, car headlights flashed on: three short flashes, three long ones, three short ones!"

"They saw our signal!" Patti exclaimed.

"Way to go!" I yelled. "They're coming!"

Chapter 9

Dr. Beekman should think seriously about entering the Indy 500 car race: He drove from the Norwoods' to Dr. Porter's house in about two minutes flat! Patti and I were standing by the gate when he roared up.

Dr. and Mrs. Beekman practically fell out of the car. Melissa wasn't with them. "What's wrong? Are you okay?" Dr. Beekman asked.

"Where are Kate and Stephanie?" Mrs. Beekman wanted to know.

We explained about the burglary, which was probably still going on, and told them about Mr. Morrell.

"Oh, dear. We asked you to keep the doors

locked! Why didn't you stay inside?" Mrs. Beekman looked so frantic that I didn't think she wanted to hear that the doors *were* locked the whole time. "Morris, please find them! Hurry!"

"The big two-story house?" Dr. Beekman pointed.

"Yes. Kate and Stephanie are hiding behind an enormous, round azalea bush," I said.

"Go back to Ira's, Barbara. Telephone the police in Ansonville." Dr. Beekman jogged toward the lake. "I'll bring the girls here," he called over his shoulder.

We jumped into the car with Kate's mom and tore back to the Norwoods'. Mrs. Norwood answered our knock. "Barbara? Where is everybody else?"

"There's a burglary going on, and Stephanie and Kate are watching it!" Mrs. Beekman said grimly. "May I use your phone?"

"Right in here." Dr. Norwood ushered her into the den.

"A burglary?" Mrs. Norwood said to Patti and me.

We nodded. "Two men are stealing furniture out of a house not far from Dr. Porter's!" Patti said excitedly.

"And one of the men is Mr. Morrell, who fixed our electricity just this morning," I added.

"Oh, my, we use him, too!" said Mrs. Norwood.

"Turn off the television, Melissa," Mrs. Beekman was saying.

"But Mom, it's *Roller Derby of the Stars!*" Melissa whined.

"Turn it off," said her mother. "I have to call the police!"

"What's all the noise?" Sam and Dave had wandered down the hall from their bedrooms.

I had to hand it to them — just by looking, there was no way you could ever tell they'd been racing around in the dark, scaring people half to death. They were wearing white T-shirts and navy-blue sweatpants, they were barefoot, and they pretended they'd been sleeping. Sam gave a big yawn, and Dave stretched drowsily.

"They ought to go onstage," I whispered to Patti.

"Um-hmmm," she murmured back. "Unless . . ."

Unless what? Who else could it have been, banging on the wall at Dr. Porter's and giggling, if it wasn't the Norwood boys? Unless . . .

"Hello . . . is this the Ansonville Police Station? My name is Barbara Beekman; I'm calling from the Spirit Lake Cottages. . . . That's right. There's a burglary in progress at one of the houses on the lake . . . a burglary. Two men are loading furniture from the house into a van. . . . Yes, about six cabins beyond Forty-nine Lake Drive. . . . A large, shingled two-story. . . . Please hurry — my eleven-year-old daughter and a friend may be hiding in the backyard. . . . Thank you.''

She smiled weakly as she hung up. ''Well, that's encouraging,'' she told us. ''I thought we'd have to wait until the police could drive out from Ansonville. But there's a patrol car cruising just minutes from here — the station notified them, and they're on their way.''

''It'll all be taken care of,'' Mrs. Norwood said soothingly. ''The girls will be fine. Can I make you some coffee?''

''No, I think we'll go back to the cabin now, to be there when Morris returns with Kate and Stephanie,'' Mrs. Beekman said.

Dave had been watching at the window. ''Look! There's the police car already! See the lights?'' His face was pressed against the glass, but over his head I could see the red light on top of the police car.

''Lauren, Patti, Melissa, we'd better hurry home,'' said Mrs. Beekman.

''Kate and Stephanie are probably going to be

in on the arrest," I murmured to Patti in the car. "We'll never hear the end of it!"

But they were inside the cabin when we arrived. "Dad made us leave too soon. We didn't get to see anything," Kate said with a sigh.

"Never mind," said her father. "What if bullets had started flying? An azalea bush wouldn't have offered much protection."

"Thank goodness you're safe!" Mrs. Beekman gave Kate and Stephanie a hug. Then she frowned at her daughter. "We'll talk about the trouble you're in for leaving the house when we're feeling a little steadier."

In a short while, a police car stopped by the house, to take our statements about what we'd seen. We told them we'd heard strange noises outside, but we left out the part about chasing the Norwoods — why complicate things? And we told about the scraping sound.

"We've had our eye on Morrell for a while," one of the officers told us. "His van had been spotted heading this way, which is why we had a car in the area."

"Caught them red-handed," said the other officer. "He and his pal were cramming one last piece of furniture into the van when the patrol car drove up. Thanks to you folks, we got them."

"Thank *you*, officers," said Mrs. Beekman, her arm around Kate.

"Make sure all your windows are closed tight," the policeman warned us as they were leaving. "Severe thunderstorms are predicted for later tonight."

"Straight to bed," Mrs. Beekman ordered when they'd driven away.

"But, Mom!" Kate protested. "It's still early! Besides, we haven't told you the most exciting — "

"We can't stand any more excitement in one evening," Dr. Beekman interrupted, and he meant it. "Get to bed, and *go to sleep!*"

We'd just climbed into our sleeping bags when a lightning bolt struck straight into the lake. Not two seconds later, there was a tremendous clap of thunder, and it started to pour.

"It's a good thing the police got to Morrell fast," Stephanie said, listening to the rain pounding down on the roof. "This'll wash away any evidence like footprints or tire tracks."

"Listen to that wind!" I said. A big gust slammed a maple branch against our window.

"Maybe the storm will uncover something in the lake!" Patti said. "I read a story once about an old

Indian war canoe that was washed out of a lake during a storm. It had been buried in the mud for years."

"Yes!" Kate exclaimed suddenly. "I read that, too. And I have a feeling something will definitely be uncovered by this storm. Something to do with Willis Pyle and Roy Jonas. . . ."

"You mean Willis's canoe?" I really wasn't ready for a ghost canoe to wash up in our backyard.

"No-o-o-," Kate said slowly. "More like Willis's money. We're going to find some coins along the shore, and we're going to turn the digging over to Sam and Dave Norwood. . . ."

"We are?" said Stephanie, puzzled. "Why would we do that?"

"Because one good trick deserves another," Kate said with a grin. "There won't really be any money. We'll just sprinkle around some of the old coins from the fireplace to make things more interesting."

"The dates on the coins are wrong for Willis and Roy," I pointed out.

"The Norwoods won't get to see them up close," said Kate.

"It just might work!" said Stephanie. "Terrific idea, Kate!"

The sound of the rain was making me very sleepy.

"I think the ghost may be with us," Patti said calmly.

"What?" I sat straight up in bed. "How can you tell?"

"Because now it's *raining* inside the house," she answered, giggling. Her bed was right under a leak!

Chapter 10

The storm knocked the electricity out again while we slept and this time there was no Mr. Morrell to fix it. The next morning we had to wash all the dirty dishes left over from dinner in boiled water from the lake!

"My hands look like boiled *shrimps*," Stephanie groaned when we were finally finished. "The ones in the cocktails — bright pink and kind of blotchy."

"I'm sure there's a recipe in your beauty book to take care of it," Patti said. "You can mix something up this evening."

We would be heading back to Riverhurst in a few hours. But we still had the Norwood boys to deal with.

"Mom and Dad and Melissa are outside," Kate said. "Let's take out the money."

Luckily the Beekmans hadn't given us a chance to tell them about finding the money the night before. We could use the coins in our super anti-Norwood scheme without endless explanations.

Kate pulled the brick out of the fireplace and grabbed the leather pouch. She jammed the pouch into her pocket and slipped the brick back into the hole. "All set," she said. "We need a shovel to make this look really good."

"I stepped on a rake last night in the dark," I told her. "Maybe there's a shovel somewhere in the front yard, too."

We came across an old license plate in the weeds, and part of a car engine, but no shovel.

"The cellar?" Patti suggested.

Success! We found two shovels and a spade, along with enough cobwebs to outfit all four of us for Halloween.

"Let's take all of the tools," Kate said. "The more of us digging, the better."

When we climbed out of the cellar, we saw Dr. and Mrs. Beekman sitting on the dock. Melissa was trying to scoop up minnows with a soup ladle.

"Where are you going?" Dr. Beekman asked

when he saw us with all the digging tools.

"Oh, we thought we'd look for Willis Pyle's treasure," Kate said with a smile.

"Good luck!" Her father grinned at us. "If you find it, I'll retire, and we'll all move to Spirit Lake."

"What a thought!" Stephanie murmured.

"Don't stay away long," Mrs. Beekman told us. "We have to start packing to go home."

"Okay, Mom," Kate replied. "Let's go this way," she said to us, setting out along the lake.

The storm had broken branches, set a rowboat adrift, even uprooted a few trees. Why wouldn't it have uncovered a treasure, too? "Where do you want to start digging?" I asked Kate.

"Dr. Norwood said Roy Jonas's cabin was three hundred feet from their property line on this side of the house. . . ."

"Which should make it somewhere near that cottage with the green trim?" I guessed. I'm terrible at picturing distances.

"Close enough," said Kate.

"But how are we going to get the Norwood boys' attention?" Stephanie wanted to know. "We could dig for hours, and they might never see us!"

"I don't think we have to worry about that," Patti said. "There they are."

Sam and Dave Norwood were standing on the end of their dock, staring in our direction — they'd spotted us, all right.

"Don't let them know you've seen them," Kate instructed. "And if they come over, be very secretive about what we're doing." She handed each of us a couple of gold coins from her pocket. "While you're digging, make believe you're snatching one of these out of the sand every so often."

"As though we've just uncovered them with our shovels," said Patti.

"Right," Kate said. We were almost directly in front of the cottage with green trim. "We've gone far enough — now I'm going to pretend I've found something on the shore."

She had one of the gold coins in her hand. She leaned over and acted as though she'd just picked it up. "Wow! A gold coin!" she screeched, throwing her arms around like someone in an old silent movie.

"Wow!" We waved our arms, too, and Stephanie jumped up and down.

"Don't overdo it," Kate muttered. "It must be Willis Pyle's treasure!" she bellowed. "Let's dig here!"

Kate had one shovel, Patti the other. They started digging like crazy, throwing sand and pebbles all over the place. I used the little spade to sift through more sand; Stephanie dug with a piece of driftwood.

"I think they're coming," she murmured without looking up. About three minutes later, Sam and Dave's yellow rubber boat bumped onto the shore beside us. The boys sat quietly in the boat, watching us as we dug deeper and deeper.

"What are you guys doing?" Sam said at last.

"Oooo!" Stephanie squealed just then. "I found another one!" She picked a coin out of the sand and brushed it off before she stuck it in her pocket.

"Shhh!" Kate hissed, looking pointedly at the boys. "Stephanie!"

Stephanie glanced at Sam and Dave, too. "Oh, sorry," she mumbled to Kate.

"What was that?" Sam wanted to know.

"What did you find?" Dave demanded. "It looked like money — *gold* money!"

"Don't be silly," Stephanie said. "Why would there be gold coins just lying on the beach?"

At that point, I pretended to have uncovered a coin myself. I jammed it into my pocket, but not before I was certain the Norwoods had gotten an eyeful. Then Patti "found" another one.

"Why would there be gold coins lying on the beach?" Sam Norwood stepped out of the boat. "Maybe because this is exactly where Roy Jonas had his cabin!" Sam started digging right next to us with his plastic paddle. "Come on, Dave!"

"Hey, you can't do that!" Kate said. "Get out of here — find your own spot!"

"Are you gonna make me?" Sam demanded. "I'll dig where I want!"

Dave had joined him with the other paddle. "Besides, it's closer to our house than to yours, so it *is* our spot!"

"You don't even *have* a house here!" Sam added. He pushed in front of Kate to start digging where she'd been digging.

Kate winked at me. "I guess there's nothing we can do about it," she said. "It's getting late. . . ."

"Right. We have to pack, Kate," I said.

"Good riddance!" said Sam. "Hey, Dave, is that a coin?" It was a flat pebble, the first of many they would find, I was sure.

Kate and Patti put their shovels over their shoulders, and Stephanie carried the spade as we marched away in a huff.

Once we were out of earshot, Kate turned to the rest of us with a big grin. "And that," she said, "takes care of the Norwoods!"

Chapter 11

"That's the last box," Dr. Beekman said, practically lying down on the trunk of the car to close it.

"Then I'm going to get started," Mrs. Beekman told him. She had shopping to do on the way home, so Dr. Beekman was driving the four of us and Melissa back in the big car. Mrs. Beekman waved and zoomed off in the VW.

Kate got into the front seat with Melissa and her father. Stephanie and Patti and I had the whole backseat to ourselves, no sleeping bags or supplies to squash us. A lot of the supplies we'd brought had been used or eaten, so there wasn't so much to take back.

"Let's see the old money again!" Melissa said as we rolled down Lake Drive.

Dr. Beekman took the leather pouch out of the pocket of his jacket and handed it to her. (We'd turned the coins over to Kate's parents when we got back from the lake that day.)

"Charlie Porter's really going to be surprised — I imagine these are quite valuable," Dr. Beekman said, glancing down at the handful of gleaming gold pieces. "Worth several thousand dollars, at least, to collectors."

"They'd look great on a bracelet," Stephanie said, holding a coin against her wrist. "Do you think Dr. Porter will sell them?"

"Maybe he'll donate them to the county historical society," Dr. Beekman answered. "They have a small museum in Ansonville."

"I can't believe it — they're still digging!" As we circled the lake, I'd caught a glimpse of the Norwood boys. They were up to their waists in a large hole, and they showed no signs of slowing down: sand was flying all around them.

"Talk about ending up in China!" Patti said, and the four of us burst out laughing.

"What was that all about?" asked Dr. Beekman.

"Oh, a little something we cooked up to get even with Sam and Dave for dunking Patti and Lauren in the lake, and for feeding Stephanie and Lauren worms."

"And for trying to scare us to death last night," I added.

"When last night?" said Dr. Beekman. "You mean at the barbecue?"

"No, after that. They sneaked out of their house after Dr. Norwood sent them to their rooms," Kate answered.

"They came over to Dr. Porter's and pretended to be ghosts," Stephanie said.

Melissa spoke up. "No, they didn't."

"How would you know?" Kate said to her little sister. "You weren't with us."

"Nope, I was with *them*." Melissa dropped the gold coins back into the leather pouch with a clink and tucked the pouch back into Mr. Beekman's pocket.

"Let me get this straight," Stephanie said. "You're saying that the Norwood boys couldn't have sneaked out after we left last night, because you were with them the whole time?"

Melissa nodded. "Until Mom came to call the police. As soon as Mom and Dad and Dr. and Mrs. Norwood sat down in the living room to talk after dinner, Sam and Dave crawled out of their rooms and lay down on the other side of the couch, out of sight, to watch TV with me." She shrugged. "They weren't so bad."

I was getting that queasy feeling again.

"Are you sure?" said her sister. "They didn't leave the den at all?"

"Not even to go to the bathroom," said Melissa. "It was the *Roller Derby of the Stars!*"

Kate and Stephanie and Patti and I looked at each other.

"Lauren!" Kate said, raising an eyebrow in warning. "It's obvious that Melissa fell asleep."

"Did not!" said Melissa.

"Did, too!" said her sister.

Did she . . . or didn't she? And if she didn't — and it really wasn't the Norwoods — then who was the extra guest at our sleepover that Saturday night at Spirit Lake?

Dr. Beekman gave the coins to Dr. Porter on Monday. Tuesday morning, Kate had a surprise for us when we met before school. "Close your eyes and hold out your hands," she said to all of us.

"It's not a worm, is it?" Stephanie asked suspiciously.

"For Pete's sake!" Kate snorted.

"Oh, all right." Stephanie held out her hand and closed her eyes. So did Patti and I.

I felt Kate put something small and hard on my palm. "Open your eyes," Kate ordered.

"The circle of stars!" Patti whispered.

"Wow! The gold coin with the Indian princess on it!" I exclaimed.

"The eagle holding the shield!" Stephanie shrieked.

"And I've got a Liberty coin." Kate showed hers to us. "They're from Dr. Porter. He's giving the rest to the museum in Ansonville."

We stashed the coins carefully in our backpacks until we could take them to the principal's office for safekeeping during classes that day.

"Something else, too," Kate went on as we pedaled down the hill toward school. "Dad's probably renting the cabin for a couple of weeks this summer, and I'm counting on you guys."

"You bet!" I said before Patti and Stephanie could even open their mouths.

One Sleepover Séance, coming up!

#7 Stephanie Strikes Back

Finally Stephanie and Kate stalked out of the building toward us.

"Well?" I asked. "How'd the Video Club meeting go?"

"Wendy and the sixth-graders are running the whole show," Kate answered grimly. "Practically all the fifth-graders walked out, they were so disgusted."

"Every time one of us made a suggestion, the sixth-graders voted it down," Stephanie said. "They were snickering about it, like it was the biggest joke in the world."

"And there's only one camera?" Patti asked.

Kate nodded. "That's all the school can afford. And Wendy'll see to it that no fifth-grader gets anywhere near it!"

"So are you going to quit?" Patti asked Kate and Stephanie.

"There doesn't seem to be much point in staying in the club, does there?" Kate replied.

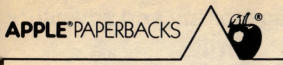

Lots of Fun...Tons of Trouble!

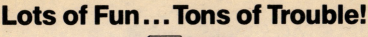

by Ann M. Martin

Kristy, Claudia, Mary Anne, Stacey, and Dawn — they're the Baby-sitters Club!

The five girls at Stoneybrook Middle School get into all kinds of adventures...with school, boys, and, of course, baby-sitting!

Join the Club and join the fun!

☐ 33950-8 .	**Kristy's Great Idea #1**	**$2.50**
☐ 33951-6	**Claudia and the Phantom Phone Calls #2**	**$2.50**
☐ 33952-4	**The Truth About Stacey #3**	**$2.50**
☐ 33953-2	**Mary Anne Saves the Day #4**	**$2.50**
☐ 40747-3	**Dawn and the Impossible Three #5**	**$2.50**
☐ 40748-1	**Kristy's Big Day #6**	**$2.50**
☐ 41041-5	**Claudia and Mean Janine #7**	**$2.50**
☐ 41040-7	**Boy-Crazy Stacey #8**	**$2.50**
☐ 41123-3	**The Ghost at Dawn's House #9**	**$2.75**
☐ 41124-1	**Logan Likes Mary Anne #10**	**$2.75**
☐ 41125-X	**Kristy and the Snobs #11**	**$2.75**
☐ 41126-8	**Claudia and the New Girl #12**	**$2.75**
☐ 41127-6	**Good-bye Stacey, Good-bye #13**	**$2.75**
☐ 41128-4	**Hello, Mallory #14**	**$2.75**
☐ 41588-3	**Baby-sitters on Board! Special Edition**	**$2.95**
☐ 41587-5	**Little Miss Stoneybrook and Dawn #15**	**$2.75**

PREFIX CODE 0-590-

Available wherever you buy books...or use the coupon below.

Scholastic Inc. P.O. Box 7502, 2932 E. McCarty Street, Jefferson City, MO 65102

Please send me the books I have checked above. I am enclosing $⎯⎯⎯⎯⎯⎯⎯⎯⎯⎯⎯⎯⎯

(please add $1.00 to cover shipping and handling). Send check or money order – no cash or C.O.D.'s please.

Name⎯⎯⎯

Address⎯⎯⎯⎯⎯⎯⎯⎯⎯⎯⎯⎯⎯⎯⎯⎯⎯⎯⎯⎯⎯⎯⎯⎯⎯⎯⎯⎯⎯⎯⎯⎯⎯⎯⎯⎯⎯⎯⎯

City⎯⎯⎯⎯⎯⎯⎯⎯⎯⎯⎯⎯⎯⎯⎯⎯⎯ State/Zip⎯⎯⎯⎯⎯⎯⎯⎯⎯⎯

Please allow four to six weeks for delivery. Offer good in U.S.A. only. Sorry, mail order not available to residents of Canada.
Prices subject to change.

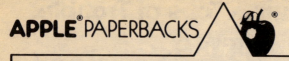

APPLE® PAPERBACKS

More books you'll love, filled with mystery, adventure, friendship, and fun!

NEW APPLE TITLES

☐ 40388-5	**Cassie Bowen Takes Witch Lessons** Anna Grossnickle Hines	$2.50
☐ 33824-2	**Darci and the Dance Contest** Martha Tolles	$2.50
☐ 40494-6	**The Little Gymnast** Sheila Haigh	$2.50
☐ 40403-2	**A Secret Friend** Marilyn Sachs	$2.50
☐ 40402-4	**The Truth About Mary Rose** Marilyn Sachs	$2.50
☐ 40405-9	**Veronica Ganz** Marilyn Sachs	$2.50

BEST-SELLING APPLE TITLES

☐ 33662-2	**Dede Takes Charge!** Johanna Hurwitz	$2.50
☐ 41042-3	**The Dollhouse Murders** Betty Ren Wright	$2.50
☐ 40755-4	**Ghosts Beneath Our Feet** Betty Ren Wright	$2.50
☐ 40950-6	**The Girl With the Silver Eyes** Willo Davis Roberts	$2.50
☐ 40605-1	**Help! I'm a Prisoner in the Library** Eth Clifford	$2.50
☐ 40724-4	**Katie's Baby-sitting Job** Martha Tolles	$2.50
☐ 40725-2	**Nothing's Fair in Fifth Grade** Barthe DeClements	$2.50
☐ 40382-6	**Oh Honestly, Angela!** Nancy K. Robinson	$2.50
☐ 33894-3	**The Secret of NIMH** Robert C. O'Brien	$2.25
☐ 40180-7	**Sixth Grade Can Really Kill You** Barthe DeClements	$2.50
☐ 40874-7	**Stage Fright** Ann M. Martin	$2.50
☐ 40305-2	**Veronica the Show-off** Nancy K. Robinson	$2.50
☐ 41224-8	**Who's Reading Darci's Diary?** Martha Tolles	$2.50
☐ 41119-5	**Yours Till Niagara Falls, Abby** Jane O'Connor	$2.50

Available wherever you buy books...or use the coupon below.